Dear Parent:

Congratulations! Your child is taking the first steps on an exciting journey. The destination? Independent reading!

STEP INTO READING® will help your child get there. The program offers books at five levels that accompany children from their first attempts at reading to reading success. Each step includes fun stories, fiction and nonfiction, and colorful art. There are also Step into Reading Sticker Books, Step into Reading Math Readers, and Step into Reading Phonics Readers— a complete literacy program with something to interest every child.

Learning to Read, Step by Step!

Ready to Read   Preschool–Kindergarten
• big type and easy words • rhyme and rhythm • picture clues
For children who know the alphabet and are eager to begin reading.

Reading with Help   Preschool–Grade 1
• basic vocabulary • short sentences • simple stories
For children who recognize familiar words and sound out new words with help.

Reading on Your Own   Grades 1–3
• engaging characters • easy-to-follow plots • popular topics
For children who are ready to read on their own.

Reading Paragraphs   Grades 2–3
• challenging vocabulary • short paragraphs • exciting stories
For newly independent readers who read simple sentences with confidence.

Ready for Chapters   Grades 2–4
• chapters • longer paragraphs • full-color art
For children who want to take the plunge into chapter books but still like colorful pictures.

STEP INTO READING® is designed to give every child a successful reading experience. The grade levels are only guides. Children can progress through the steps at their own speed, developing confidence in their reading, no matter what their grade.

Remember, a lifetime love of reading starts with a single step!

Published in the United States by
Random House Children's Books,
a division of Random House, Inc., New York,
and simultaneously in Canada by
Random House of Canada Limited, Toronto.

www.stepintoreading.com

Educators and librarians,
for a variety of teaching tools,
visit us at
www.randomhouse.com/teachers

Library of Congress Cataloging-in-Publication Data
O'Connor, Jane.
The teeny tiny woman / retold by Jane O'Connor ; illustrated by R. W. Alley.
    p.   cm. — (Step into reading. A step 2 book)
SUMMARY: A teeny tiny woman, who puts a teeny tiny bone she finds in a churchyard away in
a cupboard before she goes to sleep, is awakened by a voice demanding the return of the bone.
ISBN 0-394-88320-9 (trade) — ISBN 0-394-98320-3 (lib. bdg.)
[1. Ghosts—Folklore. 2. Folklore—England.]
I. Alley, R. W. (Robert W.), ill. II. Title. III. Step into reading. Step 2 book.
PZ8.1.O24 Te 2003 [E]—dc21   2002013448

Printed in the United States of America   54 53 52 51 50

The Teeny Tiny Woman

Retold by Jane O'Connor

Illustrated by R. W. Alley

Random House 🏠 New York

A teeny tiny woman
lived in a teeny tiny house.

One day she put on
her teeny tiny hat.

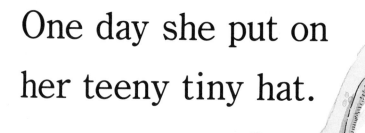

She got her teeny tiny bag.

And she went for
a teeny tiny walk.

Soon the teeny tiny woman came to a teeny tiny gate.

She opened
the teeny tiny gate
and went into
a teeny tiny yard.

There she saw
a teeny tiny bone
on a teeny tiny grave.
"I can make some
teeny tiny soup
with this teeny tiny bone,"
said the teeny tiny woman.

The teeny tiny woman
put the teeny tiny bone
in her teeny tiny bag.

She went through
the teeny tiny gate.

She walked
and walked
and walked
all the way back
to her teeny tiny house.

The teeny tiny woman

opened her teeny tiny door.

"My teeny tiny feet are tired,"
said the teeny tiny woman.

"I will not make
my teeny tiny soup now."

The teeny tiny woman
put the teeny tiny bone
in a teeny tiny cupboard.

Then she got into
her teeny tiny bed
for a teeny tiny nap.

Soon a teeny tiny voice called:

"Give me my bone!"

The teeny tiny woman
was a teeny tiny bit scared.

"I must have had
a teeny tiny dream,"
she said.

The teeny tiny woman
had a teeny tiny glass
of milk.

Then she got back into
her teeny tiny bed.

Soon she fell asleep.

It was not long before
the teeny tiny voice
called out again.
"Give me my bone!"

The teeny tiny woman
woke up.

She was so scared
she hid under
her teeny tiny covers.

But the teeny tiny voice
called out again.
And now it was not
teeny tiny at all!

The teeny tiny woman
peeked out from
her teeny tiny covers.

She said,

"TAKE IT!"

And that is the end of
this teeny tiny story.